THIS BOOK BELONGS
TO

Budgee Budgee Cottontail

Written and illustrated by Jo Mora in 1936
Printed in Hong Kong
Designers: e design, Ketchum, Idaho

First Edition

Published by

Dober Hill Ltd.   an imprint of

STOECKLEIN
PUBLISHING

Post Office Box 856
10th Street Center, Suite A1
Ketchum, Idaho 83340
(208) 726-5191

Budgee Budgee Cottontail

by Jo Mora

Dober Hill Ltd.   *an imprint of*

STOECKLEIN

PUBLISHING

Ketchum, Idaho

The Jo Mora Collection

Stoecklein Publishing is proud to bring *Budgee Budgee Cottontail* out into the wide, wide, world for the very first time. Also available: authentic reproductions of Jo Mora's original classics, *Trail Dust and Saddle Leather* (ISBN #0-922029-18-0) and *Californios* (ISBN #0-922029-19-9), smyth-sewn and case-bound in hardcover, with every effort to replicate the original editions; and *Jo Mora, Renaissance Man of the West* (ISBN #0-922029-20-2), an illustrated biography by Steve Mitchell. All three books are available separately or together in a commemorative slipcover case (ISBN #0-922029-21-0).

To my father,
for writing the book he always
dreamed of writing.

— Jo N. Mora, Pebble Beach, California, 1995

Publisher's Dedication:

To Jo N. Mora of Pebble Beach, California, son of Jo Mora, for keeping *Budgee* safe for almost sixty years, and finally releasing him out into the wide, wide world. Also to Patty Mora, daughter of Jo Mora, who made her brother promise to do it.

And to the children, parents and teachers of Ketchum, Idaho; Salinas, California; and Rye, New York for their support and enthusiasm.

—David R. Stoecklein, Ketchum, Idaho, 1995

nce, in a cottage ivyclad,
With brothers, sisters, Mom and Dad,
Right at the end of the forest trail,
Lived Budgee Budgee Cottontail.
He longed to travel from what he'd heard
Of the wide wide world from the old Jaybird.
But Mom said, "Goodness gracious, no!
The Wolf gets Bunnies that wander so."
To change his mind he tried a lot,
Though the harder he tried the worse it got.
'Til early one morn, at the break of day,
He tiptoed out and hurried away.

hile skipping along he soon passed through
His well-known woods to where all was new,
And the trail uphill to a sign-post led:
OUT TO THE WIDE WIDE WORLD were
The words he read.
And there, old Grandpa Spider, too,
Wiping his web of the morning dew,
Crossly grumbled, "You'd better go home.
No place for you out there to roam.
Go back and mind your Mom and Dad."
But Budgee laughed, "You're just too sad.
My mind's made up, and that is that."
And the angry Spider screamed, "You brat!"

way went Budgee tramping along,
Out in the sunshine, singing a song,
'Til late in the day, ringing loudly and clear,
A crackety-crack! in the woods he could hear.
And there at a nutcracker built on the ground
A busy old Squirrel was what Budgee found.
He was scared to fits when Budgee popped into view,
And scolded and screamed such a hullabaloo
That he raised all his neighbors who swarmed about
The tops of the trees and joined with a shout,
Pelting poor Budgee with everything near.
And wasn't he glad when he got in the clear.

Ill-treated, hungry, sore, and sad,
That first day out was very bad.
But good luck came next morning when
He found a cabin in the glen.
There, with her babies on her back,
Biddy O'Possum cooked a snack
For Budgee's breakfast, in a while,
Of sweet potatoes Southern style.
Then, "Here's a bundle," she did say,
"To bring you joy upon your way."
Yummy, yummy, things to eat;
Cornbread, molasses, what a treat!

tartled from his nap that noon,
Came these words from a fierce Raccoon:
"For lunch a Bunny — not so bad."
And Budgee said, "Well, I'll be glad
To make your meal quite something new,
With cornbread and molasses, too."
Well, how that Coon with joy did roar.
Yet Budgee added, "Something more:
Count fifty slow with tight-closed eyes,
And I'll give you the big surprise."
The greedy Coon did that and say,
Did Budgee Budgee run away!

cross the woods to open land,
He then heard Foxhounds close at hand;
Jumped in a cave, 'twas black as night,
Saw two big eyes — a scary sight.
Then came a growl, "They'll catch us now
If you don't run out and tell them how
The Fox just left, without a doubt.
Go quick!" and Budgee stumbled out.
"A big red Fox just left!" screamed he,
And crossed the field to that tall tree."
"He did?" asked one, "Then no delay.
Come Pups, let's go!" and dashed away.

JO MORA

udgee Budgee, what a scare!
The Hounds were gone, but, standing there,
Bushy tail, red, tall and slim,
Another creature grinned at him.
"I'm Reddy Fox, on this depend,
You saved my life, now I'm your friend."
So off they went, a friendship rare,
Fox and Bunny, what a pair.
Reddy taught him many tricks
To save his hide in any fix.
But Foxhounds found them one fine day,
And each one ran a different way.

ow, lonesome Budgee wandered on
'Til in the woods he came upon
A funny cabin opened wide,
With tempting carrots hung inside.
He took a bite — zam! whango! clap!
And there was Budgee in a trap.
A Lynx peeped in, eyes all aglitter,
Said, "I'll be back with friends for dinner."
He left, and then, at Budgee's toes,
The ground heaved up; out popped a nose.
"I'm Uncle Abner Mole, young chap,
Why goodness me, you're in a trap!"

ell, Uncle Abner dropped from sight
And yelled, "Quick, all you Moles, unite!
Come, hurry here!" when, strange to say,
By scores they came without delay.
They dug that hole 'til large enough
For Budgee, with a huff and puff,
To squeeze down through; no time to spare,
For the Lynx came back and then and there
They clawed inside to no avail,
Just missing Budgee's cottontail.
"That Bunny's ours." The answer came,
"Not while Abner Mole is my name!"

bner Mole then said, "I fear
The Lynx will now stay camped right here.
We'll have to ask the Fairy Queen
For help to get you out unseen."
When word was sent, she did not wait,
But drove right up in coach and eight.
She said, "This seed now quickly eat
And then these words you must repeat:
Hocus Pocus Alakazee
Make me as small as I'd like to be."
This he did, and glory be!
No bigger than a Mole was he.

nother seed, new words to learn,
When back to size you would return:
Hocus Pocus Alakazam,
Make me as large as I really am.
And now be gone, 'tis getting late.
You'll get new orders at the gate."
Through the longest tunnel they went by choice,
'Twas dark as pitch, then heard a voice,
"Get on my back, I'm Honka Goose.
There now, we're off. Grip tight the noose."
Away they flew and saw below
The watching Lynx by the campfire's glow.

ll night he flew, when, dizzy and spent,
He dozed; let go; down Budgee went!
Hung up in a bush, caught on a limb,
And a big-eared stranger laughed at him.
"Bad Jack Rabbit, that's my name.
Wolves and Grizzlies, they're my game.
I smoke out Wildcats from their nest.
The one-gun terror of the West."
Just then another popped in sight
And snarled, "Well, Bad Jack, here's your fight.
I've got a knife; you draw your gun.
Wild Pete Coyote craves the fun."

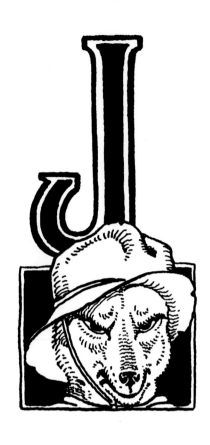

ack dashed away with all his speed,
And Budgee laughed, "Now watch this seed.
'Twill make me large, though now I'm small."
But the magic words he could not recall!
"That's hocus pocus," Pete replied.
"Why that's just it!" our Budgee cried.
"Hocus Pocus Alakazam,
Make me as large as I really am."
Presto chango! Gave a yell,
And scared, Wild Peter ran pell-mell.
"Phew!" sighed Budgee, breathing free,
"I'd like to know where I may be."

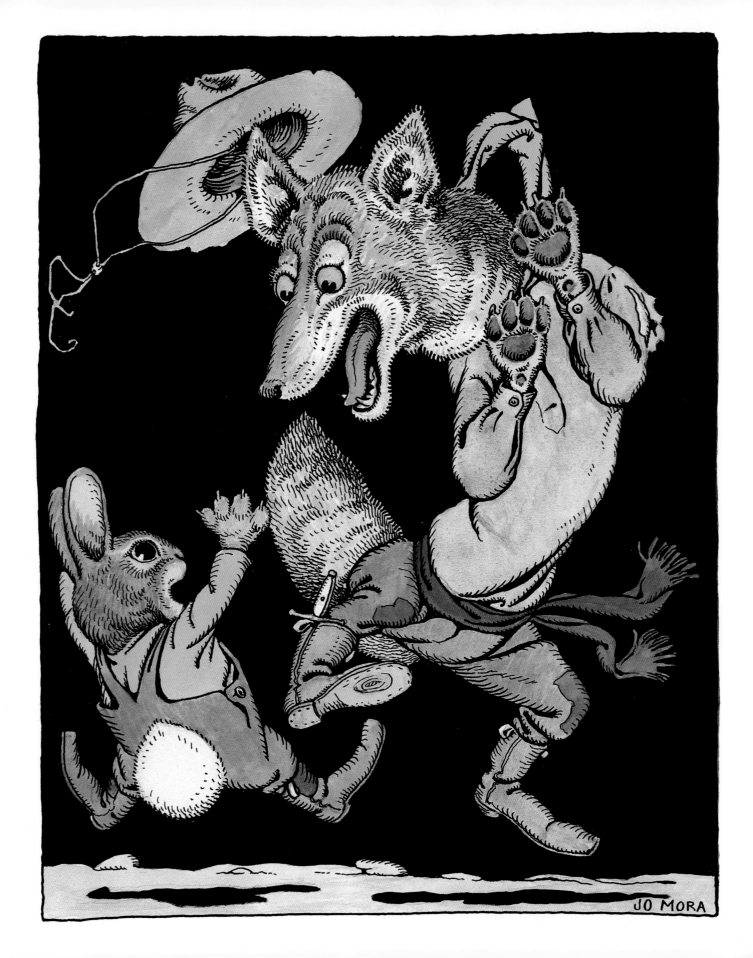

hile playing with a butterfly,
An Indian Pony colt skipped by.
Pinto Fleetfoot was his name.
Then Budgee told him from where he came
And wondered how he could return.
So, to his Daddy, proud and stern,
The colt took Budgee for advice.
"Ugh. Heap bad medicine, not nice."
"Aw, be yourself, Dad," Pinto said.
He answered, "Story books me read
Make heap big Injun talkum so."
And Pinto sighed,"Well, you should know."

ow, Pinto's Dad, though stern, did say
He'd help our Budgee on his way.
They put him on a Pony and
Away he rode to Burroland.
There, such a jolly clown he met,
Called Happy Pancho Burro, yet
No one in all that land could cope
With him to spin or throw a rope.
And soon our Budgee, quick to learn,
Was roping everyone in turn.
'Till he and Pancho, just for fun,
Kept all those Burros on the run.

T omorrow we'll begin to roam,"
Said Pancho, "heading you back home.
The going's tough, the scenery strange
Across the Texas Longhorn Range."
So over hill and deep ravine,
Seeing much yet never seen,
In twenty days of traveling fast,
Cow Ponyland they reached at last;
And met two friendly Buckaroos
With chaps and spurs and long lassos,
Named Blazeface Luke and Sorrel Top.
Then Pancho left, he could not stop.

hen Luke said, "We will show you how
We throw a rope to catch a cow."
But when our Budgee said that he
Could throw a rope, they roared with glee.
"All right," cried Budgee, "watch me cast."
Pulled out his rope and spun it fast,
Jumped right through, then snapped it clear
Catching Blaze Face by the ear.
Well, what a hit he made with that.
Then Sorrel Top gave him his hat
And laughing said, "Now that makes you
A first-class Bunny Buckaroo."

JO MORA

n time, more ponies came that way,
When all hands left without delay,
With whoops and shouts and fun no lack
As Luke took Budgee on his back.
They traveled far — six days went by —
Then came to mountains rough and high.
Alone then, Budgee, winter near,
Commenced his climb with little cheer;
When, resting on a canyon rim,
Two great big Bears pounced down on him,
And scared him so he could not budge.
But they just yelled, "Wow! Here's the judge!"

e our judge, and just watch out
To keep us straight in a wrestling bout.
And if we bite and scratch and scuff,
Jump in between and treat us rough."
Just think of it — 'twas really funny —
Fighting Bears bossed by a Bunny.
They clinched; then clawed and chawed until
They bounced high rolling down the hill.
But up-trail Budgee puffed and went
'Til, out of breath then, scared and spent
He stopped to rest, when, tall and trim,
A Buck in buckskins sat by him.

ucky heard sad Budgee's woe,
Then said, "I'll pass you on to go
By Bighorn, Goat and Musk-ox back
To Snowshoe Rabbitland, then smack
To Santa Claus 'til he can leave
To make his rounds on Christmas Eve."
"Oh, great stuff, Bucky, you're a dream
To think up such a dandy scheme."
Then, like on springs, they climbed and ran;
Met Tommy Bighorn; told him their plan.
Up climbed Budgee. "So long, Buck!"
And off like a rocket run amuck.

rossing high mountains and canyons wide,
What a ride, oh, what a ride!
Running, jumping, sailing high,
With many thrills six days went by.
Then, on a peak ahead, did note
Friend Uncle Billy, Mountain Goat.
When asked his help, he laughed, "Ho, ho!
You betcha boots, jump up. Let's go."
Then came more thrills over a dizzy trail,
To beat the winter or they'd fail.
Skies now grew dark; snow was at hand;
But soon they came to Musk-oxland.

inter came with storms of snow,
Yet Oompah Musk-ox said he'd go.
Eye-kee, the Beaver, lent his aid
With a suit of furs all tailor made.
A shiny gun made Budgee bloom,
Cut from the handle of a broom.
They went for days with much to fear
For white Wolves often crowded near.
But reached their goal quite safe and sound,
And there a Snowshoe Rabbit found
Named Tip Tip Tippy Toes, and who
Declared he'd see our Budgee through.

ell these two Bunnies started forth
To their journey's end in the frozen North;
And safely reached that happy place
Where Snowbirds greet and Reindeer race.
Budgee's adventures were complete because
This was the home of Santa Claus.
Happy ending, timed just right
With Christmas Eve that very night.
Busy Santa merrily
Hugged them both and begged to be
Excused, yet asked a wrinkled Gnome
To help the Bunnies feel at home.

uch sights they saw. Such fun they had.
Scores of Gnomes at work like mad
Packing up the toys and things,
Hobby-horses, dolls and rings,
Skates, hoops, sleds and pop-guns dandy,
Bags and bags and bags of candy.
Though all in Santa's sack did go,
It never seemed to overflow.
More Gnomes were polishing the sleigh,
While milk-white Reindeer munched their hay.
Then, bread and jam — they ate a heap —
And by the fireplace fell asleep.

Budgee woke up with a fright
A Gnome was shaking him by torchlight.
"Santa's calling! Time to go!
Put on your furs and don't be slow."
He dressed; dashed out; Oh, what a sight!
A hundred Gnomes waved torches bright.
"Jump in," cried Santa, "All aboard!"
The Reindeer plunged, ran fast, then soared
Up in the skies, while "Cheerio
And Merry Christmas!" rang out below.
They skimmed the moon, then, snuggling deep,
A dizzy Budgee fell back to sleep.

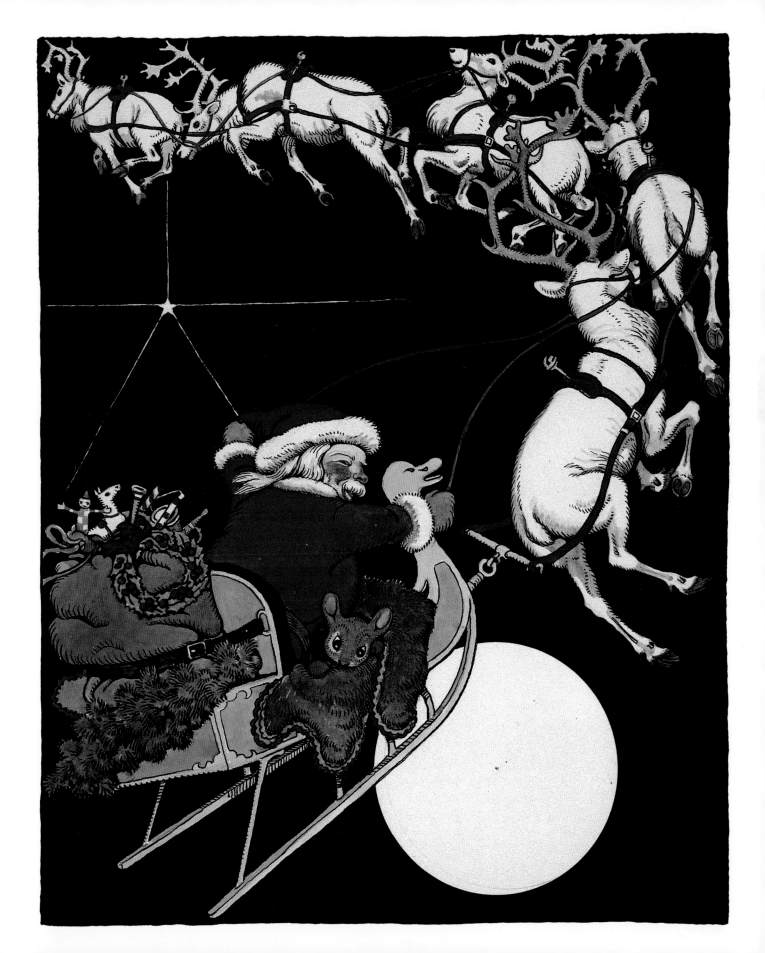

hen he woke 'twas the end of his ride.
A white beard on him, Santa tied,
Then let him down the chimney fast,
And there was Budgee home at last.
Mom thought him Santa and, at sight,
Cried, "Where's my wandering Bunny tonight?"
Off came the whiskers, "Budgee's here!"
Then what a shout, what joy, what cheer.
Of the wide wide world and adventures great
They listened to stories 'til awfully late.
And Budgee sighed when in bed tucked tight,
"Merry Christmas to all and to all a Good Night."

Glossary

Bighorn: Rocky Mountain sheep that live high up in the roughest sections of the mountains. These animals are very sure-footed, which helps them walk, run and stand on rocky, high peaks. Bighorn sheep are a dark beige or tan color with white hips and rumps. They have large, thick horns that curve up and back over their ears and down, around and back up past their cheeks in a "C"-shaped curl.

Buck: The male deer of the "Cervidae" family, which includes deer, elk, antelope and moose. Male deer, or "bucks," are powerful animals who have sleek, sandy-colored fur and big, solid horns or antlers. Bucks shed, or lose, their antlers in late winter, but they don't go without antlers for very long. Their antlers begin to grow back right away and first appear as velvet, which is the soft covering of the growing antlers. This velvet then hardens into the full-grown antlers by late spring.

Buckaroo (buk'-a-rew): The old California word for cowboy. He was a man who could bust a bronco (break or tame a wild horse) and who wore fancy, colorful Spanish gear and clothing. The word buckaroo came from the Spanish word "vaquero," which means "Mexican cowboy."

Chaps: A pair of leather leggings with wide flaps worn by cowboys and cowgirls to protect their legs. The word is an abbreviation of the Spanish word "chaparejos" meaning leather leggings. Chaps are worn as protection while riding horseback through sagebrush and cactus, against rain and snow, and when a horse tries to bite the rider or brush him against a fence or other animal.

Coach and Eight: A large, four-wheeled carriage that is pulled by eight horses, or in this case, eight beetles!

Foxhound: A special dog that is bred and trained for hunting foxes. These hounds are medium-sized with either black and tan, black, tan and white, or tan and white coats (fur).

Hullabaloo (hul'-uh-buh-loo): A clamorous, or noisy, sound or disturbance. Lots of uproar, commotion and excitement.

Ivyclad (eye'-vee-clad): Something, like a house, that is covered with ivy. Ivy is a green shiny vine plant that clings to objects and climbs as it grows.

Longhorn: This fierce, nearly extinct English breed of beef cattle has an enormous spread of horns that is sometimes six or more feet! The longhorn was the wild kind of cattle brought to Mexico in the 1500s. They crossed the Rio Grande and roamed up to the Red River, which now separates Texas and Oklahoma. The first longhorns were driven, or herded, by cowboys to New Orleans, California and Colorado. The old-time cowboys loved the longhorns because they put up a such a good fight.

Lynx (links): A member of the cat family with long, silky fur, fuzzy tassles on their ears and furry feet that help them walk in soft snow. Lynxes like to swim in lakes and rivers, and climb high up into trees where they rest and wait to leap on passing prey.

Mole: A small animal with velvety fur, very small eyes and strong front paws that are used for digging holes in the ground. Moles live underground and eat insects.

Musk-ox: A large, buffalo-looking ox with shaggy fur hanging down nearly to its feet. Musk-oxen weigh from 400 to 900 pounds! Their large horns are hollow and curve down close to the sides of their heads, then out and up to pointed tips. Musk-oxen can see and hear very well, and they can run very fast if they have to. These large animals live in a herd of 3 to 100.

Noose (nooss): A loop with a knot that tightens as the rope is pulled around something, usually an animal's neck or head. This is used to lasso, or catch, a cow or horse.

Opossum (oh-poss'-um): A small, mousy-looking animal the size of a house cat. Opossums have long, furless tails, short legs and large, naked ears. They often hang upside-down in trees with their tails wrapped around a tree branch. The female opossums have a pouch on their bellies where they carry their babies. When in danger, opossums roll over, shut their eyes and pretend to be dead.

Range (rānj): A large stretch of open country; a large grassy plain; a vast area of unfenced land used for grazing animals, usually cattle.

Ravine (ra-veen'): A very deep, narrow, steep-sided canyon or valley that has usually been eroded, or worn down, by running water.

Sorrel (sor'-ul): A horse that is a light chestnut, or reddish-brown color with a light blond-colored mane and tail.

Swarm (sworm): To move about or gather around in great numbers. Bees swarm together in their hive. People swarm together at an exciting event like a baseball game or a rodeo.